Death by Airship

Death by Airship

Arthur Slade

ORCA BOOK PUBLISHERS

Library and Archives Canada Cataloguing in Publication

Slade, Arthur G. (Arthur Gregory), author
Death by airship / Arthur Slade.
(Orca currents)

Issued in print and electronic formats.
ISBN 978-1-4598-1870-5 (softcover).—ISBN 978-1-4598-1871-2 (pdf).—
ISBN 978-1-4598-1872-9 (epub)

I. Title. II. Series: Orca currents
PS8587.L343D43 2019   jC813'.54   C2018-904693-7
                             C2018-904694-5

First published in the United States, 2019
Library of Congress Control Number: 2018954153

Summary: In this high-interest novel for middle readers, Prince Conn must
solve the mystery of who is killing off all the heirs to the pirate throne.

*Orca Book Publishers is dedicated to preserving the environment and has
printed this book on Forest Stewardship Council® certified paper.*

Orca Book Publishers gratefully acknowledges the support for its publishing
programs provided by the following agencies: the Government of Canada,
the Canada Council for the Arts and the Province of British Columbia
through the BC Arts Council and the Book Publishing Tax Credit.

Edited by Tanya Trafford
Cover artwork by Shutterstock.com/Melkor3D
and Deviantart.com/struckdumb
Author photo by Black Box Images/Jerry Humeny

ORCA BOOK PUBLISHERS
orcabook.com

Printed and bound in Canada.

22   21   20   19   •   4   3   2   1

This one goes out to
Aargh and Aaargh and Mom.

Chapter One

If you smell smoke, don't panic!

My father, Pirate King Jules, used to say that all the time. Usually when he was sitting on his throne of bones, lighting his pipe.

But chances are, if you're standing on the deck of a creaky wooden airship two hundred fathoms in the air and you smell smoke, you're going to panic.

I was on the deck of my airship, *Cindy*. And I did smell smoke. A poop deck full of it. And the panic struck me right to my rotten pirate core. My beloved ship was on fire, and my crew of hardy cutthroats was looking at me for instructions.

"What be your orders, Prince Conn?" Bonnie Brightears asked. Her ears were indeed bright, a glowing red from constant sunburn. Forty years in the sun will do that. She'd been on nearly every type of airship used to traverse the twelve seas—she knew her stuff. Bonnie was my quartermaster, the second in command. Her red ears really set off the blue in her coat.

I didn't let anyone see the panic on my face. I only allowed my little toe to tremble. They wouldn't spot that through my leather buccaneer boots. In my fourteen years of life, I've learned a lot about how hearty, cutthroat crews react to panic. I watched my dad deal with them. And my mom.

It's always best to keep a stiff upper lip. *Only let your little toe panic*. That was Mom's favorite saying.

I knew that if the flames traveled from the aft deck and ran up the rigging to the sails, we were in big trouble. If they continued to climb up to the giant whale-shaped, bladderlike balloon atop *Cindy,* we'd be seeing more fireworks than New Year's Eve night on Skull Island. Heck, the resulting explosion would be visible across the One Hundred and One Islands—Dad's whole kingdom.

I imagined most of my brothers and sisters would clap with happiness at the sight of me going down in flames. Not that they're all mean, but they do like a good show. Only Bob, eighth in line to the pirate-king throne, wouldn't clap. He gave up pirating to be a librarian. We're all so ashamed of him.

Anyway, the explosion would be mega big, because there's hydrogen in that whale-shaped balloon. Hydrogen is lighter than air, and it keeps us airborne. But when fire meets hydrogen, it gets messy.

I'm talking no-survivors, blow-us-all-up messy.

"Any orders for the engine room, Captain?" That was Odin, the sailing master. His pale skin was sunburned and pitted with scars. His jacket was bright orange, he was missing an eye, and, as usual, he'd tied daggers in his red beard. Our captives found it intimidating. But he mostly just used the knives to cut up his ham at dinner.

"I'm going to have a nap in my cabin," I said. "Then I'll take a look into this problemo." I was attempting to sound cool and calm. I'd been captaining the ship since I was twelve. They still didn't get my extremely clever sense of humor.

"We don't be having time for that!" Bonnie exclaimed. Her ears glowed. "We be on fire, Captain!"

She was right. Bonnie was always right. Except when it came to grammar, but pirates hate grammar! The flames were up the rigging now and had leapt to the sails.

I thought I saw a dark spot in the distance. Another airship perhaps? But there was no time to grab a spyglass. Whatever it was, it was beetling away from us.

We didn't have any large reserves of water on the ship—no more than a few pails of drinking water. Nor could I afford fancy fire extinguishers. Because I am ninth in line for the throne, when it came time to hand out ships and equipment, all I got were the dregs. That includes my airship *Cindy,* much as I love her. My oldest brother, Reg, flies *Dragonslayer*. My oldest sister, Bartha, soars on *Crusher*, and, well, you get the picture. *Cindy* is 82.5 percent airworthy.

There was plenty of water below us though. We were sailing over a large empty patch of Aargh Ocean (the Imperial Forces of Angleland, long may their ships burn, had a longer Latin name for it—but we pirates spit at their names. And at their Latin. They rule the nearest continent and see us as pesky flies). The obvious thing to do would be to crash into the sea. Doing so would more than likely douse the flames and save our lives.

But there was a big kink in that plan. Not one of my hearty crew could swim, including me. Pirates are notorious for not knowing how to swim. And we're too brave to have lifeboats. Maybe *brave* is the wrong word. *Cheap*. We do have one launch boat, but it has a hole in it. Getting Odin to fix that is on my to-do list.

"Tighten the aft sails, wing the yardarm and batten the hatches!" I shouted. Then I ran to the ship's wheel. It was smooth wood, with a few broken spokes.

"What we be prepping for?" Bonnie asked.

"It's going to be a surprise," I said. And that was no lie. I had no idea what to do and had just shouted those orders to keep everyone busy.

I grabbed the wheel tightly, preparing to take action. What kind was not clear yet. Evasive action wouldn't work in this case. What to do?

My mind drew a blank.

Then it drew another blank.

Make that three blanks.

"Captain!" Bonnie shouted. "We be needing more orders!"

But I had nothing.

And then the answer came to me. It was one of those crazy, death-defying

7

answers that me and my brother princelings and sister princesslings used to come up with when we were kids. It had worked every time when we played in the Bone Palace on Skull Island. We'd used our toy airships to execute the maneuvers. Of course, we had a good grip on them. And we only lost half of our hand-carved crew.

I glanced back. The problem was the flames. They climb. Upward usually. And these flames were climbing to the top of the sails. And licking at the bottom of the airship bladder.

We were moments from exploding.

"All hands on deck!" I shouted. "Anchor your booties! Lash yourselves to the yardarm if you have to."

Bonnie repeated my orders. The entire crew started securing themselves to the decks. They had better do it quickly, I thought, because there wasn't much time. I stepped into the metal bands in front of the steering wheel, and Bonnie clamped them over my feet. Then she grabbed a rope.

"Now hang on!" I shouted. I am embarrassed to say my voice creaked a little. Puberty! It's not for the faint-hearted. Then I pushed the lever ahead and we went into a full dive, straight toward the ocean. Bonnie was shouting something, but the wind was whistling so loud that I couldn't hear. It was something like, "Do you be insane, Captain?" When we were only a few yards from the water and certain destruction, I cranked the wheel and hit the after rudders. *Cindy* turned sideways, then slowly flipped upside down.

Like I said, my plan had been theoretical until that point. I saw Bonnie staring up at me. She was hanging by a rope. The others also were holding on tight.

Now, cranking an airship upside down is a great way to make things fall out. A cannon broke away from its moorings, bounced off the bladder and splashed into the water. Thankfully, we had tied our anchor, so it couldn't create drag in the water.

I pushed the wheel a bit forward, until the top of the balloon just touched the water. Skimming along the surface. Another push, and it was deeper in the water. Waves formed on either side, and they began splashing up the sides. Higher. Higher.

I gave the wheel one last good push, and the whole ship began to vibrate. The water splashed even higher, finally reaching the flames. I glanced behind me, because the flames were burning up the ropes now. I dug a little deeper, despite *Cindy*'s creaking and shivering and shaking. The balloon and the ropes holding it were strained to their very limits. At any second the balloon could rip off and leave us trapped underwater.

Fifty drowned pirates and a dead parrot.

But a giant splash found the last flame. I cranked the wheel, and we flipped upward slowly, oh so slowly. I thought we might end up stuck in the water on our side. But the fantastic *Cindy* gave another shudder.

The right side came down. The bottom, that is. We were upright in the water, and the fire was out.

My crew burst into spontaneous applause. Even Hooky, who has a hook for a hand, applauded. He said, "Ow, ow, ow" the whole time.

Don't clap your hands when you have a hook. It's an old saying.

"Roll call!" I shouted.

Bonnie yelled out the crew names.

"Aye!"

"Aye!"

Fifty living pirates. And one dead parrot. (Did I forget to mention that my parrot, Crackers, had died two weeks earlier from eating gunpowder and a match? There were a lot of feathers to clean up.)

There was also one burned-out arrow.

Odin discovered it wedged into the aft mast. Someone had shot a flaming arrow right into our ship. I thought back to that dark spot I'd seen in the sky. The arrow could only have come from another airship. But if that had been a ship, it had been very far away. A shot would have been nearly impossible from that distance.

There was only one person I knew who could make a shot like that. My sister Bartha.

It was time to pay her a visit.

Chapter Two

There were repairs to do first, of course. Bonnie, Odin and Hooky looked after getting the rest of the crew to do the work. That is, after several of them cleaned out their breeches. A few of the ropes had snapped, but we had plenty of rope. And our spare sails (our only spares) were soon attached to the rigging by pirates climbing like monkeys up and down the main mast.

I ate some salted cod and drank lemon juice, to keep the scurvy away. Man, I would have killed for a banana. We'd been roaming for a fortnight, and our fruit stores were gone.

At noon a white dove landed on the sail and made a cooing noise. My heart leapt, and I did a jig for joy. Not because I'm a birdwatcher or because I particularly love doves (although they do taste good in a stew), but because I know only one person who uses hunter-seeker doves like this.

A moment later a shining white spot appeared in the sky, with white wings that swooped on either side. It was a one-person swan boat, aptly named *Swandiver*. And the balloon keeping it aloft was also as white as snow.

It winged its way down to us and pulled alongside. The young occupant, who was blond and had the fairest skin in all the pirate islands and the three continents, was dressed in an ivory-colored dress. She gently tossed her anchor across and then gracefully walked along the extended gangplank. She was holding a rather large silk bag.

Crystal is her name. She is fifteen years old, and we are dating.

Well, I'm not quite sure *dating* is the right word. *Almost dating* would be more accurate. She took a liking to me after I shared notes with her in Pirate Ethics class. She is studying to be a nurse in Stitch-Me-Up Island. It's a sanctuary where anyone with a wound in their mind or body can go to be fixed up. It's the one place no pirate or pirate-hunting Imperial ship will ever attack. It's run by Edith Mack, a blind woman who can still stitch up twenty pirates or soldiers a day. Like I said she's blind to your past and present— her only goal is to keep people together.

Crystal had taken the ethics class with me because it is important that nurses be able to understand pirate language and customs so they don't hurt their feelings while they are attaching peg legs or strapping on eye patches. I had promised to show her the pirate life from the inside out. She'd get extra credit for that.

And I'd get extra time with her.

The dove landed on her shoulder. The whole cutthroat crew took a deep breath at the perfect beauty of that moment. It was like a painting come to life.

"I finally found you," Crystal said. "I've been looking everywhere for you, Prince Conn. For a week."

"We've been roving," I said.

She hugged me, and I hugged her back, even though it had been some time since I'd showered. She smelled like cinnamon.

Just to let you know, even though we've been almost dating for a while now, we've never actually kissed.

Not yet.

"And how has your pirating been going?" she asked.

"We captured a tea vessel and a salt ship and a toy ship too."

"Toy ship?"

"I mean a ship full of toys." I pulled a figurine out of my pocket. It was a girl in a wedding dress on a boat. I'd known as soon as I saw it that Crystal would love it. I handed it to her.

"I love, love, love, love it," said Crystal. She was very excited about everything in life.

I've never been to Cloud Island, where she grew up. All I know about it is that it is very far away. And that there are lots of clouds there. And bananas.

I mention that detail because when she lowered the bag she was holding, dozens of bananas, oranges and apples tumbled out. "I thought you might appreciate these," she said. "I brought enough to share."

The cutthroats let out a hardy "hip hip hooray!"

"You are so very kind to us," I said.

"You and your crew are my special project. Especially you." She sniffed. It was a very beautiful sniff. There wasn't even the slightest gurgling of snot. "I smell smoke."

"Smoke? Oh, nothing to worry about. Just some pirate stuff. I will be taking care of it really soon."

"A full stomach of fruit will help with getting pirate stuff done," she said. Then she sniffed again. This time there was only the slightest snoogling of snot. It still sounded heavenly.

"Have you seen any amazing sights lately?" she asked.

I did watch Odin playing ping-pong with his glass eye, I nearly said. Then I remembered that ladies probably don't like that sort of talk. "I have seen some amazing sunsets. They were very, very..." I searched for a romantic word. "Sunny. Err, but they got less sunny as they set. And the color red was involved."

"Oh, that does sound divine. Perhaps someday we could watch the sun set together." Crystal glanced up at the sun. "Well, I must be going now. I have Lower Gut Wounds class in a few hours." She reached in for another hug. I puckered up my lips just in case, but she managed to avoid them. Instead she kissed the air a few inches away. An almost kiss. "Don't forget our plans for a picnic lunch on your birthday," she said.

Then she was back on the swan ship. And swanning away.

All the cutthroats watched her go, swooning away.

"Get back to swabbing the decks!" I shouted.

"Swab the decks!" Bonnie repeated. "We be swabbing hard!"

We met in seventh grade. Not Bonnie and me, but Crystal and I. The same year I got *Cindy*. Crystal had been impressed to meet a real pirate prince. I'm pretty sure she's still impressed.

By high noon the rigging was fixed. I have to admit, this crew is made up of mostly good, strong and hard workers. "Captain Conn," Bonnie reported, "we be fully repaired at 82.5 percent."

Well, the ship couldn't get better repaired than that. "Then set the tack for the northeast," I said. "I want to pay my sister Bartha a little visit. Full speed ahead."

Thankfully, we had good winds. Our steam engine was acting up again.

Odin promised to have it fixed again by the next day.

We climbed higher and higher. It wasn't long before the smell of smoke was blown off the ship. I went from spyglass to eyeballing the horizon to spyglass to compass.

After about three hours I spotted Break Bones Island and Bartha's tree house. By tree house, I mean a gigantic tree mansion made up of more than twenty rooms, built in a tree that reaches out of the earth like the hand of a giant. The morning was cool, and there was lots of fog rising up from the ground and clinging to the tree house itself. Right at the top was the dock. Big enough to hold several airships at once.

I could see through my eyeglass that *Crusher* was docked. Good. "Come straight out of the sun," I commanded. We climbed up and up and then tipped the front of the ship, flattened the sails and rocketed down out of the sun. My hope was that they wouldn't see us until the last moment.

Princess Bartha is second in line for the throne. She isn't the delicate kind of princess. She knows how to use a cutlass better than anyone. And she can swear like a, well, like a pirate. She is not someone you should ever underestimate.

"Powder the guns!" I shouted. My cutthroat crew obeyed. "Raise the flag!" They raised the Prince Conn flag, which bears the skull and crossbones and a pickle.

Yes, a pickle. Like I said, I got last choice when it came to the pirate gear. But at least it was a pickle with an eye patch.

No one messes with the pickle!

Only as we got closer did I see that the tree house had already been smashed. Clearly it had been under attack recently. There were cannon holes here and there.

And what I'd thought was fog was actually smoke. The drawbridges lay broken, a whole floor made of bamboo was in tatters, and Bartha's flag, the skull and crossbones and a single red eye, was smoldering.

"Full stop!" I shouted. We swooshed up the sails and dropped anchor. It caught the top branch and jerked us to a stop.

"Bring *Cindy* in close!" I shouted.

We swung alongside the dock, and I jumped the gangplank and landed on the creaky wood. I'd been here many a time in the last few years. Bartha is a pretty good big sister, and she makes rather good brownies. I rushed up the stairs to her main quarters and burst through the door. Odin and Bonnie were right behind me.

The front room is where Bartha keeps her doll collection. The dolls are made of clay, and each one is missing its left eye. Bartha did that on purpose, and then put an eye patch on each doll. But now I could see that someone had broken every one of their clay heads. As I stepped into the room, the floorboards creaked, and several of the dolls said, "Mommy, mommy, mommy."

That really creeped me out. I used to be unable to fall asleep when they were in the same room as I was. But today I sped past their broken bodies.

I kicked open the doors of my sister's observation room.

Bartha was leaning up against the wall, a white dressing bandage across her chest and a flintlock pistol in her right hand. She pointed it straight at me. Her skin, usually quite tanned from all her days in the skies, looked quite pale. The blood seeping through the bandage might have had something to do with that. I motioned for Odin and Bonnie to back off.

"Hey, sis," I said.

"Hey, traitor," she said.

"What does that mean?" I slowly put my cutlass away. There was no point bringing a cutlass to a flintlock fight.

"You sabotaged my boat, and you attacked my tree house. And you killed my parrot!"

Her emerald-green parrot, Poxonyou, was lying at her side. Dead. She'd been a good bird.

"I'm very sorry about Poxonyou," I said. "But I didn't do any of those things!"

She pointed down with her left hand. Her right held the gun steady, despite her wounds. "Your victory flag is planted in the ground."

I glanced out the window and looked down at the beach. There were twelve skull-and-crossbones-and-pickle flags waving in the sand. They did look rather impressive.

"But it wasn't me!" I said. "*Cindy* doesn't have that kind of firepower."

"You hired out. Found more cut-throats."

"I have no reason to. I swear, Bartha, I didn't do it!"

"You're seventh from the throne now." She said this in an accusatory fashion. "When I die you'll be sixth."

"What do you mean? I'm ninth!"

"No," she said. "Clint is dead."

Clint? My brother Clint is fourth in line to the throne—or, at least, he *was*.

I pictured his rugged face. It had become rugged because he won fistfights by using his head as a battering ram. Nothing could kill him. "How? What happened?"

"As if you don't know!" she barked. "Poisoned. By a pickle, no less. That was *so* creative."

"What? I don't poison people with pickles!" I spat this sentence.

"You're the quiet type. You'll do anything," she said with a sneer.

Again, I want to point out that the gun she had aimed right at me was not wavering.

I did some quick math. "Wait! If I'm seventh from the throne now, who else died?"

"Tressa! Her ship blew up and crashed into the water. Sabotage! Probably an exploding pickle. All they found amongst the floating broken boards were your pickle playing cards and a tattered flag."

Not Tressa. She had a great heart. And she was always so kind. Except for that time she broke my arm when I beat her at blackjack. "I did not do these things!"

"I don't believe you." Bartha clicked back the hammer. "And with one flick of my finger, my last act will be to end your attempted reign of terror. Right here. Right now."

A bead of sweat ran down my forehead. My toe began to tremble. Violently.

She pulled the trigger.

Chapter Three

Pffft.

That's the sound the flintlock made. Like a gun-sized fart. No round ball came shooting into my brain.

Did you know that gunpowder doesn't work well when it gets wet?

Bartha looked at the gun, shook it, pushed back the hammer with her left index finger, pointed and pulled the trigger again.

PFFFT.

She rolled her eyes, then threw the pistol at me. She was weak from her wounds, so it landed at my feet.

"Now you can kill me and be sixth from the throne," she spat. "Well, go ahead, bro. But first I will cast my final pirate curse." It was a curse that all pirates have. It doesn't often work, but it makes us feel better as we die. "I curse you to dwell down full fathom five in Davy Jones's locker, where the crabs will nibble on your toes. And other extremities."

I didn't like the sound of that. Especially the "other extremities" part.

I put my hands on my hips. "I'm not going to kill you."

"Oh, torture first? Great. You're so predictable. Bring on your worst pickles!"

"No. I'm not going to torture you! Or maim or poison you or even snap your eye patch. Or squirt pickle juice at you. I didn't do any of those things you accused me of."

My sister stared at me for a long moment. Well, several moments. Then she sighed. "Sorry, Conn. I really did think it was you. You have a shifty look in your eyes."

What did *that* mean? But I didn't snap at those words. Instead I took a deep breath and said, "It's okay. I'll take your suspicion as a compliment. I am a pirate prince, after all. And I really am sorry about Poxonyou."

"She saved my life. 'Duck, duck, duck!' she shouted. And I ducked. A cannonball took off my pirate hat. And took Poxonyou too." Bartha looked like she was about to shed a tear. But she sniffed loudly instead. "Still, one of their snipers got me when I was issuing commands. A darn good shot." This time she huffed out a wheeze. "Well, I think I'm going to die now."

I looked at her wound. The redness near her stomach didn't seem to be growing any brighter or bigger. I motioned, and Bonnie Brightears came closer. She took a medical kit out of her leather fanny pack. She got to work and within seconds held up a round ball of shot. She gave me the thumbs-up.

"You aren't going to die," I said.

"Yes, I am," Bartha said. "I can feel it coming." She looked around, then closed her eyes. She opened them again a moment later. "Actually, now that you have that bullet out of me, I'm feeling slightly better. Maybe the pain I'm feeling now is sausage gas."

Bartha *does* like bacon-flavoured sausage. She'd poked me in the eye once just so she could steal some from my plate.

Bonnie finished treating my sister's wound. It takes a lot to kill a pirate princess.

"I guess I won't die," Bartha said. "I'm kind of disappointed actually. I'd prepared a long final speech."

"Well, save it for next time. As Mom often says, be prepared for death, because death is prepared for you. Anyway, you should take it easy."

"I'm fine." She tried to get up, then fell back down on her rump. "Maybe I'll just stay seated."

"I'll get you to Stitch-Me-Up Island. And then I'm going to hunt around and figure out who attacked you."

Bartha pointed at me. "Good luck, Pickle," she said. Personally, I hate the nickname. She must have seen the look on my face. "I mean, good luck, Conn.

Be careful. Someone really sneaky is trying to bump us all off."

Then she closed her eyes. Bonnie made a motion, and two of my crew came in to transport my sister. They'd row her on one of the smaller boats to Stitch-Me-Up Island and then catch up with us.

While I had been talking to my sister, my hearty crew had already been up and down the island, looking for clues. No one had spotted a thing. I went down to where the pickle pirate flags were flapping.

I grabbed one. Checked out the flagpole. It was a normal wooden one. Then I studied one of the flags itself. It was a very good copy of the original. Someone had taken the time to deliberately frame me for this. Imagine how long it must have taken to make all these flags. Well, no sense in wasting them, I thought. I would get my crew to gather them up for the next time we returned to Skull Island with a hold full of bounty. Flags would make our arrival look so much more cool.

I looked closer at the bit of silk. Generally, seamstresses are proud of their work. And sometimes they sign it. Their initials can often be spotted somewhere, be it a hankie, a pair of underwear pantaloons or a flag.

There were two initials on the back of the flag, in the bottom corner. P.P.

Patricia Pandora.

I knew the name well. She had been my kindergarten teacher at pirate school.

Chapter Four

I have fond memories of pirate kindergarten. They were the best three years of my life.

That's a joke. It only took me two years to finish kindergarten.

We gathered together on *Cindy—mustered* is the correct word, but my crew gets hungry and starts thinking of hot dogs whenever I say that. We had found a store of dry gunpowder and a collection of cannonballs. Which was good, since during our last battle we ran low and were shooting pots and pans from our cannons. Not exactly effective or frightening. And it made our cook pull his hair out.

It had been about ten years since I'd last seen Mrs. Pandora. I knew she'd moved from Pirate City on Skull Island to a small village on One Tree Island. So we upped our anchor and set sail.

The island really does have only one tree, and it's a pine tree, of all things. There aren't that many pine trees in this part of the world, so people there make the most of it. Every Christmas they have a huge celebration, and presents for every villager appear under the tree. It might be a way to get people to move there. It worked on Mrs. Pandora—she went there after she retired and opened a seamstress business in her home.

We landed next to the tree. Bonnie and Odin slid their cutlasses into their belts, and Odin adjusted his beard daggers. They made to follow me off the gangplank.

"Hey! Hey!" I said. "You don't need to come with me this time."

"With all respect due," Bonnie said. She had her hand on her pistol. She had named it Eye Squasher. I'd never asked her why. "She be dangerous, I bets."

"She's my kindergarten teacher!" I said. "She taught me how to make paper snowflakes. And happy-anniversary cards."

"Just the same, Sir Captain Conn"— Odin was always so official—"we should come along. Maybe put a cannonball through her hut first."

"You will not be blowing up my kindergarten teacher's home! I forbid it. Walk around the village. Scrape some barnacles off the ship. But stay away from Mrs. Pandora's house."

Odin didn't say anything, but I could tell from his face that he wanted to argue. So did Bonnie. She opened her mouth.

"That's an order," I said.

Their faces became even harder stone.

I left them standing there like statues. I marched down the gangplank and through the village to Mrs. Pandora's shop, Little Sew and Sew. Clever name! She worked out of her home, which was a large hut made of bamboo, with a grass roof. There were all sorts of sample flags for every member of the royal family on the outside wall of her hut, including my pickle flag. I guess people collect them.

I knocked on the door. No answer. I knocked a second time.

Mrs. Pandora had tried to teach me the difference between right and wrong, a hard thing for pirates to learn. But I was pretty sure it would be wrong to kick down her door.

So I snuck in through the window. Problem solved. She'd be very proud of me.

It was dark in that hut. I wasn't familiar with the layout, and my eyes hadn't adjusted. I shouldn't have been surprised when I knocked over something made of clay.

It was breakable.

And loud.

"Umm, Mrs. Pandora, are you in here?" I asked.

The answer was a blow to the head and a kick to my rear quarters. Something else made of clay or porcelain broke. My eyes were starting to adjust. I turned and received a foot to the jaw.

I blocked the next blow and counter chopped the one after that. You see, I'd learned kung fu from Mrs. Pandora.

It had been one of the best classes in kindergarten.

My opponent was dressed in black, with a black bandanna. All I could see of his or her face were burning, angry eyes. I drew my cutlass with great style, but my hand was smacked, and the sword flew through the air and stuck in the wall. I had no extra daggers. Or even a thumb tack. I was disarmed. My least favorite way to be.

I remembered Odin's idea of putting a cannonball through the hut. I should have listened. I hoped they could say, "I told you so" later.

I just had to survive.

But I wasn't sure I would. Because my opponent was good. Like, nasty good.

I attacked with a double-fisted strike and found myself upside down and flying through the air. I landed on a wicker chair. It collapsed. I was struck with another blow on my backside.

And then another blow, which I blocked. I was blocking every second one. And every first one hurt. Really hurt. I couldn't seem to successfully mount an attack of my own.

I was knocked into another room. A room with a window. And the light from outside fell on me.

"Prince Conn!" my opponent cried out. It was a woman's voice.

I looked up. The masked face stared down at me, the eyes showing shock.

"That's me," I said. I tried to stand but found I couldn't.

My attacker pulled back her black mask. It was Mrs. Pandora! She was seventy years old if she was a day, but she had just turned me into princeling mincemeat.

"Welcome to my house!" she said. "Would you like some lemonade?"

Chapter Five

"I had no idea it was you." Mrs. Pandora reached out and pulled me up. She was as strong as any twenty-year-old. She set me on a chair and somehow came up with a glass of lemonade. Which I sipped. It was to die for.

"I didn't know it was you. But why were your eyes so angry and red?" I asked.

"Oh, I just haven't had my coffee yet. Why were you sneaking into my home?"

"No one answered my polite knock."

She gestured at her clothes. "Well, you just happened to arrive while I was doing my exercises. That's why I'm dressed like this. And maybe I was a little hyped up. There are too many wannabe pirates here. Would you like some cookies?"

All I could do was nod. My noggin hurt. My shins hurt. My spleen too. She handed me a a plate of oatmeal-chocolate-chip cookies. After I ate one I felt much better. I'd loved cookie day in kindergarten.

"So what are you doing here?" she asked. Then she paused. "Oh, and how did you like that order of flags? It really was some of my best work. Did your birthday party go well?"

"Birthday party?" I asked. I took another sip. Boy, did Mrs. Pandora ever make good lemonade. "I didn't order the flags. And I didn't have a birthday party. Never do. They're bad for morale. It's best not to remind my cutthroat crew how young I really am."

"Well then, we better talk," she said.

"Who ordered the flags?" I asked.

"The flags were ordered by royal decree."

"Royal decree?"

She got up and opened a file. "Yup. I've got it right here," she said, pulling out a little tube. I recognized the official royal orange paper. "Stamped by the ruler himself. Your father, King Jules."

I unrolled the roll. An order direct from the palace for fifty pickle flags in celebration of the fifteenth birthday of Prince Conn.

Signed by my father. Well, it was just an *X*, but he had a very distinctive *X*.

Shiver me timbers! Could my father really be behind this? It was hard to believe. For one thing, he never celebrated my birthday. Or anyone else's. For another, did he have the smarts to plan an attack on Bartha and make it look like mine?

Yep. He could. One didn't become pirate king without having a brainpan full of smarts.

"Could this have been faked?" I asked.

"Everything can be faked," Mrs. Pandora said. "But I am certain this is the royal seal. I've seen this skull-and-crossbones insignia several hundred times. I'm a kindergarten teacher, don't forget. I recognize these things. It's my job. The stamp is real."

Well, this would take some thinking to figure out. "And how were you paid?"

"The payment came by royal carrier pigeon." She looked at me. A mysterious glance. "What is with all these questions? Is there something I should know, Conn?"

"Nothing," I said. "Family squabble."

"Oh," she said. "Well, those are not all that rare, are they?"

She was right about that. My father had wrested the throne from my uncle Boris, who had wrested it from his own father. So far, we siblings had been doing our best not to do any wresting. Maybe Dad was trying to make sure that didn't happen. He was a friendly old cuss as long as you followed orders.

Unlike his sister, Zeba—my aunt. Now she was a piece of work. A one-eyed pirate who had tried to take the crown from Dad, and by that I mean she blew up half of Skull Castle with her ship (which has the aggressive name *Die! Die! Die!*) and stormed the top keep with a hundred hired Amazon pirates (they come from Amazon Island

and tend to keep to themselves unless you pay them enough gold). Aunt Zeba had come close to winning that day. But at the last moment my mother had swooped in, blasting Aunt Zeba's ship with her mighty guns. With well-aimed shots Mom knocked over the mast, punctured the balloon and cracked the rudder.

The *Die! Die! Die!* had limped away with Dad in pursuit. The ship crashed into the water and exploded with the loudest *BANG* I'd ever heard, and my aunt Zeba, her daughter and the Amazon pirates drowned in the deeps. This all happened on my fifth birthday. All I remember thinking was that there were a lot of fireworks for my birthday.

"What are you thinking about?" Mrs. Pandora said.

"Oh, just fondly remembering our family get-togethers. We don't have enough of them." I threw back the last of my lemonade. "Thank you, Mrs. Pandora. It was nice to see you, but I really should be going. There's loot to get. Ships to seize. The usual."

"You have a good work ethic," said Mrs. Pandora. She always was such a positive teacher. "Wait, I have a gift. I've been meaning to give it to you since you got your first ship. Actually, it's for your crew too."

She went into a back room and returned with a sack. I looked inside.

"Wow. This is very kind of you," I said. "Extremely kind." I closed the bag. "I'll wait for just the right moment to give this to the crew."

"Actually, I hope you never have to," she said. She took my hand, then wouldn't let it go. Her hand was warm. And strong. "Is there anything else you want to tell me? Perhaps I could be of some help. I don't mind giving my students advice."

I shook my head. I really didn't want her worrying about me. "It's okay. I just wanted to pop by and say thanks for the flags." I hoped she would forget my comments about fake documents. "My birthday celebrations are going to be amazing. I can't wait."

I had just lied to my kindergarten teacher. You shouldn't be surprised.

I am a pirate, after all.

Chapter Six

Cindy rose up into the sky with all the smoothness of a bucking moose. But we were off. And I trusted her to get us to our destination. I'd taken the bag Mrs. Pandora had given me and put it in the cabin behind my treasure chest. I was hoping I'd never have to open it again.

I stood in front of the steering wheel

and stared at it. It was time to make our way to our destination.

If only I knew what that destination was.

"Where we be going, Captain?" Bonnie asked.

I'd told her everything I'd learned from Mrs. Pandora, though I skipped the part where my kindergarten teacher had bested me in battle. To explain the bruises I told Bonnie I had slipped and hit my head.

"Well, if my father is somehow behind the attack on Bartha and the deaths of Tressa and Clint, our best bet would be to get a load of coal, fire up the steam engine and sail as far away as we can."

"That be running," Bonnie said. "That be cowardly."

"That be exactly what it is," I said. Part of me wished she'd just said, *Good idea, Captain Conn*. "You're right.

You're right. But the more I think about it, the more I realize that Dad wouldn't bump off his kids. He's mean. But not paranoid. And he's so strong, everyone is afraid of him. Besides, I'm his favorite." I paused, remembering the time he'd shot me with the salt gun. "Well, I think he has a soft spot for me, at least. He's only shot me once."

"But they be using the royal seal. It be a palace plot."

"You're right. That means someone in the royal castle is involved. They've stolen the seal. Or are making orders without my dad knowing. It might be Mom. She's shot me twice and even poked me with her cutlass."

"You think she be planning this?"

"Well, she does have a temper. And Amber is her favorite, so Mom might be gunning for her to have the throne. Amber is sixth in line." Then I paused and counted on my fingers. "No, she's

53

fourth in line. That's still a lot of gunning to get her to the top." Then I remembered my mom stroking my hair when I was frightened. One time she'd given me a teddy-bear pirate when I'd had a nightmare about my ship crashing. Or maybe it was about skeletons attacking us with swords. Anyway, the usual pirate-kid nightmares. "But Mom really doesn't seem the type. And she does love Dad. And most of her children."

"So who be it then?"

"I guess it could be Brutus. He's always been so loud. He likes owning things. But the only thing he seems really passionate about is hunting Imperial ships. And Reg is already first in line, so what would be the point in implicating me?"

"Well, I be stumped," Bonnie said.

"Whoever it is, they're a good planner. And great at keeping secrets. Maybe it's one of Dad's generals."

Just then a dove landed on the main sail and cooed. My heart leapt at the sight of it.

Swandiver appeared in the sky again.

Fireworks went off in my heart. Oh, wait, never mind. It was some of the men testing the cannon. The others lined up as Crystal boarded the vessel in her white gown. Except Bonnie. She backed up. I had seen her do that before. But I ignored her. She was probably trying to give us our privacy. Well, as much privacy as you can have with your whole crew around you.

"You're safe!" Crystal said as she rushed toward me and gave me a big hug. "I heard about your sister. And your brother, and your other sister, and your other brother."

I did the math. I broke the hug. "My other brother?"

"Yes. I must admit my mom is a bit of a gossip. I came as soon as I heard.

I'm talking about Brutus. Didn't you hear? He has fallen into a volcano."

"A volcano?" I said. "But Brutus is the best pilot of all the princelings and princesslings!" He is my second-eldest brother. And he is built like a brick outhouse. But he doesn't smell like one. I just want to make that clear. And he is smart. He is a fox in the sky.

"I-I don't know much about your... business in the skies. But the Imperial Navy tracked him down and chased him. Right into the volcano. His ship exploded. All crew lost."

"But he was the best at hiding. He knew every airship-sized cave in the One Hundred and One Islands. How could they ever find him?"

"There is a rumor going around that someone put a smoke marker in his ship. Easy to follow. Hard to hide. It let out a pickle-green smoke."

"Pickle-green smoke?" My mind whirled. Someone was still trying to frame me! "I can't believe it."

"I am so sorry to be the bearer of bad news. Here. I brought you some more fruit. And cookies."

The pirates let out a cheer. They had heard every single thing we'd said. There's no privacy on a pirate ship.

"Oh, and a gift just for you," Crystal added. She pulled something out of the bag she was carrying. It was a shirt made of green silk. The color of a pickle. With the wide collar and puffy arms that all pirates love. I nearly wept at the beauty of it.

"You are so kind," I said, a bit overwhelmed. Then Crystal leaned toward me. I thought we were finally going to kiss. But at the last moment she kissed her own palm and put it on my cheek.

"*Awwww!*" one of the crew yelled. I couldn't tell which one, but I'd figure it out. He would soon be swabbing the latrines until his nostril hairs burned out from the stink.

My cheek was on fire. "You take good care of yourself, Conn," Crystal said. "I don't know what I'd do without my pickle-pirate hero." She whispered this last part so no one but me could hear it. Never had I heard such a lovely turn of phrase.

"Yeah, you too. Bye," I said. Ugh! I am so bad at this sort of thing.

She turned and floated toward her swan ship (or, at least, it seemed that way, because her dress covered her feet). The wings of the ship spread, and then Crystal was gone.

Pickle-pirate hero. I would be dreaming about that phrase all night.

Chapter Seven

I snapped out of my fog when I remembered that another one of my siblings was dead. Brutus hadn't been the kindest of brothers, but he'd been tough and he'd been my hero. I couldn't believe that the Imperial Navy could even catch up with his ship, *The Majestic Grouch*. (That was Mom's nickname for him when he was little.) And now he and his ship and crew had all gone up in flames.

Bonnie was at my side again. "What be your orders, Captain? Where are we headed for?"

I only paused for a moment. Bravery and a bit of anger were making my heart and my head strong. "We're going to get to the bottom of this by going straight to the top—right back to the palace. Set coordinates for Skull Island. Full speed ahead."

"It'll be pushing her to the limit," Odin said. He was playing with one of the knives in his beard. "But the steam engine can take it, sir. I've tightened all the quadulators."

Sometimes Odin just makes things up. I made a mental note to look up *quadulators* in my *Pirate's Guide to the Guts and Bolts of Your Airship*.

Bonnie barked a few orders at the crew. Her voice was louder than thunder. Then she turned and said in her quiet voice, "We don't know what we be finding there."

"There will be great danger," I said. Oh, and I said this bravely. "But we laugh at great danger."

"Oh, the great danger it be left the boat," Bonnie said.

I looked at her with confusion. "The only person who left the boat was Crystal."

"I be saying nothing more."

"You don't like her?" My voice squealed a bit when I said this. Puberty!

"Oh, she be a delicate flower. I be not mattering about her. But I be not liking how you act around her. It be un-pirate-like."

Bonnie is old enough to be my mother. She comes from the old stock of pirates. A long line of quartermasters. Her father was my father's quartermaster before an octopus pulled him into the ocean.

He went screaming, "I can't let calamari kill me!" But it did. Which is funny and sad at the same time. He did manage to poke out one of its eyes though.

Anyway, there are specific ways we are supposed to act as pirates. One is to not show any emotion.

I let my little toe deal with the emotion.

"Well, I don't want to hear that kind of talk again," I said. "That's an order. And I'll have you know that I'm always pirate-like."

"I be quiet, Captain Conn, sir," she replied. Bonnie almost sounded bitter. Maybe she was getting crazy. Or scurvy. I noticed she hadn't eaten any of the fruit. I offered her a cookie from the bag.

Bonnie put up her hand. "I be gluten intolerant," she said. And off she went to do her quartermaster duties. Which was yelling at pirates to swab the decks. And picking who was on latrine duty.

I went to the wheel, opened my compass, looked at the sun and set our course at heck bent for leather toward my father's palace on Skull Island.

We were currently well east of that place. Each of King Jules's children had been given their own territory in the One Hundred and One Islands to patrol. Mine, of course, was the farthest away and the least populated. There wasn't a lot of trade in the area. That meant not too many merchant ships to pirate, so I didn't have much treasure in my hold. Dad always asked, *How's the ship? Anything in your hold?*

I had a more pressing problem than disappointing Dad. I'd be crossing the territories of my siblings, and that was like racing through a crocodile pit.

"Put up the green flag of friendliness," I said. Bonnie echoed the command. It's fun to give out commands. Though some commands, like "Scratch my stinky feet," don't seem to work. There are some things a scurvy crew just won't do. Once the flag was flapping, I felt safer. It's a sign to all pirates that our guns will be silent and we won't be pirating their skyways. They get sensitive about that.

We crossed my sister Morgana's territory, and I held my breath in fear. Her ship is called *Sharkeater*, and she is particularly accurate with her long-distance cannons. She also has a grudge against me. You see, as a child I once stole her toy pirate doll. She mentions that theft every time we meet, but insists she's forgiven me. Odd thing is, every Christmas I find each of my presents has been pinned to the floor by a dagger. Thankfully, no one's given me a puppy.

I breathed a sigh of relief when we were out of her airspace. I stopped glancing left and right and up and down like a turkey looking for the ax-wielding farmer.

As we sailed through Brutus's airspace, I felt a sadness in my heart. There were black sky rowboats of mourners already gathering to grieve. There would be an official funeral in three days. Three funerals coming up. Maybe more.

When we were past his section of airways, I let one tear run down my cheek, thinking of my lost siblings. Brutus. Clint. Tressa.

And then a cannonball went clear through our deck. Alarm bells rang. It was Bonnie ringing them. "Get to your battle stations, you scallywags!" she shouted.

I stared at the smoking hole. It was only a few feet away from my toes. From me!

I raised my spyglass and looked out into the skies. It's the oldest trick in the book to come out of the sun.

Just to the left of the sun (pirates are smart enough to not look directly at the sun—except for Blinky Bill) I spotted it. A huge shadow of a ship. Its guns were blazing.

I nearly started crying again.

It was the *Vengeance*. My mom's ship.

And through my spyglass I could see very clearly that she was the one standing at the wheel.

Chapter Eight

"It's Mom!" I shouted. "It's Queen Athena!"

"We be doomed," Bonnie whispered. For she knew as well as I and the rest of the crew that my mom, Athena, has the second-biggest and baddest ship in the whole pirate kingdom (Dad's ship *Goliath* is first). And her crew was firing all guns at once. Heavy-metal thunder was coming toward us.

"Incoming cannon fire!" I shouted. A ball tore through the sails. Another knocked our rowboat out of its moorings. And the third punched another hole in the deck. Fortunately, none had hit the giant bladder of hydrogen above us, or we'd have been diving earthward.

I just like saying the word *bladder*.

Anyway, I had some barking to do. "Evasive maneuvers!" I shouted, which translated to Odin putting more coal in the fire. I grabbed the steering wheel, turning us this way and that, watching cannonballs fly over us, fore, aft, port and starboard.

The Vengeance is much, much bigger than *Cindy*. She has about a hundred more guns. And with two giant steam engines, an air paddle and sails made of non-rip silk, she can travel a lot faster. We were doomed. Doomed. Doomed!

But we continued to dodge most of the cannonballs. The crow's nest was knocked askew and stood at an angle. Our spotter was barely hanging on. "I be fine!" he shouted.

"She be gaining on us," Bonnie said. "And she be looking steaming!"

I glanced back. *The Vengeance* was now directly behind us, not falling for any of my maneuvers, and Mom, dear sweet Mom, was clearly aiming right at me.

I'd never seen her this mad. Even when I scribbled on her favorite treasure map. Which, um, meant she never found that treasure again.

I saw her raise a bullhorn to her lips. "Stop your boat!" she shouted. "That is an order from your Queen. And prepare for boarding, you traitorous killer scum."

"Should we be stopping?" Bonnie asked.

"No! She looks too mad," I shouted, continuing to turn *Cindy* this way and that. "But maybe, *maybe* I can talk her down. I'm good at that." Actually, I'm not, but I didn't want to admit to the crew that I had no other plan.

"And prepare for a summary execution," my mom added.

Gulp. Even though *summary* made me think of schoolwork and essays, I knew she meant the deadly way. The off-with-his-head way.

Me. Her ninth child, her baby boy. Cute little Conn.

Mom never messed around when it came to executions.

"Stop the ship or you will all soon be dead!" she shouted.

"I be thinking she means it," Bonnie said. "What be your orders?"

"I am not sure I can talk sense into her. She's super mad at me for *something*," I said. "Do you remember me doing anything wrong?"

"I be not remembering that. You be not sending a birthday card. Maybe that be it."

"That doesn't deserve an execution! Or being tagged as a traitor!"

"You have ten seconds to stop the ship!" Mom began to count, lightning fast. "Ten, nine, eight, seven, six…"

"What be your orders, sir?" Bonnie shouted. "Orders!"

I couldn't think of any.

"Five, four, three, two, one. *FIRE!*"

"Dive!" I commanded. And we dived.

Sometimes you get lucky. And sometimes you don't.

We got lucky. *The Vengeance* overshot us, both with her cannons and her bulk, and dropped down, gaining speed as we turned to head in the opposite direction of Mom.

And that's when our second piece of luck happened.

Our rudder snapped.

Now that may not sound lucky, but because it was broken it flapped back and forth, faster than I ever could have controlled it. *Cindy* shook, shuddered and darted left and right. It was impossible to follow us. I could still hear my mom yelling, "Traitor! Traitor! Traitor!" on the bullhorn.

The ship was in danger of shuddering into a thousand pieces. The wheel was useless. We were out of control. Creaking through the sky. *Cindy* cracked and crawed. But *The Vengeance* was no longer in pursuit.

"We've escaped!" I shouted. I nearly did a dance.

"Yes," Bonnie said. "But we be flying madly. Someone will have to fix the rudder."

"Sounds like a job for Big Hands Joe," I said. He really did have big hands.

A small guy, smaller than me, and wiry. But he could hold on to anything.

We got out the lowering device—a really thick rope—tied it to his ankle with a double knot and lowered Big Hands Joe down the side of the ship. He had a hammer in one hand and a bolt in the other, and when he reached the rudder he banged the bolt into the bolt holder on the rudder.

The rudder was fixed. We let out a cheer. And every single pirate on the ship applauded.

Which was a mistake, because someone let go of the rope, and Joe fell.

But he does have big hands. He used the empty one to grab a cannonball hole and climb back into the ship.

"Put some extra ham in his supper," I commanded.

Now we were sailing straight again.

In the wrong direction. Away from the palace. Away from answers.

Away from danger.

"Should we be turning around?" Bonnie asked.

Chapter Nine

It took me a while to reply. In fact, I didn't have the answer. "Let's run through what we know. My sister Bartha was attacked. Brutus fell into a volcano. Clint ate a poisoned pickle. Tressa's ship exploded. I have no information on Reg, Amber, Morgana or Bob. Clues leading to me were found at every scene."

"Hey! That be meaning you're now sixth from the throne," Bonnie exclaimed, counting on her fingers. "Congrats!"

I didn't feel happy about it. "Yes, there's that. But the person who did this has access to the royal seal, can buy the loyalty of fleets big enough to attack Bartha and has inside connections to the Imperial Navy. And for some reason is blaming it all on me."

"Don't be forgetting your mom. She still thinks it be you."

"How could I forget? My dear ol' mom tried to blow me—well, all of us—right out of the sky. While calling me a murderer and a traitor."

The safest thing to do right now was to keep sailing away. We could rebuild the ship and then find a way to reach out. Maybe I'd try a message in a floating helium bottle.

But then again, we should face the problem head on. That was the pirate way. "I want to solve this mystery right now. So we should fly like the wind. Or maybe fly in the wind. To Skull Island."

"It be certain death," Bonnie said.

"One thing is certain: death is not certain until it's certain." I got that from a pirate philosophy class I took. I'm sure my teacher would be proud.

And so it was that *Cindy* began limping through the skyways and airstreams toward Skull Island. Toward the home of my family, a hearty band of cutthroats that was getting smaller by the minute. Toward, perhaps, the traitor or traitors framing me for all these murders.

When I was about twenty leagues by sea from the island, a dark raven winged out of the sky and landed on the yardarm. It was wearing a crown.

The king's raven.

It was a message from Dad. Or, if he was dead now, which was entirely likely, then it was from whoever was in charge now.

I walked carefully toward the raven, who eyed me with suspicion. It had kind of an I'll-peck-your-eyes-out look on its face. I started to reach slowly for the little tube on its leg but changed my mind. This could be a trap.

"Hooky," I said. "Will you get the message for me?"

"Yes, sir, Captain Conn." Hooky was a cheery sort. He went up to the bird as if he were approaching a child, whistling all the way. Maybe the whistling calmed the bird. Or maybe it just liked the look of Hook. Anyway, he was able to reach in with his hook and pull out the metal tube.

"By hook or crook, I got it," Hooky said. He did enjoy his puns. (So did his father, Salty Stu, who had died when he got trapped in quicksand on Quicksand Island. His last words were *I have a sinking feeling*.)

I motioned for Hooky to pass me the tube, so he hooked it to me. I opened the tube, pulled out the scroll and broke the royal seal, the same one I'd seen on Mrs. Pandora's flag order. I unrolled it gingerly. And nervously.

Prince Conn,

You are hereby summoned to an audience with your father, King Jules, ruler of the One Hundred and One Islands (and the airspace around them). You must come at once to the palace. Alone. Without arms.

The southern path will be a place of safe passage. I promise no harm will come to you. Pirate's honor.

Signed,

Pirate King Jules

I showed the scroll to Bonnie. She stared at it for a second and then said, "I can't read, sir."

"Oh. That's right," I said. "I keep forgetting."

So I read it to her.

"Pirate's honor? Southern path? He be sounding serious. Do you think your mom knows about this?"

I shook my head. "I bet it's a secret message. He wants to meet with just me. But what I don't know is why."

"Maybe he actually be believing that you are not a traitorous blood brother and blood sister betrayer."

"Perhaps. And with the route he suggested, we should be able to travel safely. It would be a relatively easy flight. Maybe we'll get some answers."

"What be your orders, Captain Conn?" Bonnie asked.

I think she knew the answer. "Let's

take the southern quadrant. I really want to get to the bottom of this."

I forgot that it's really bad luck to say that if you're a pirate. We don't like getting to the bottom of anything. Because that means your ship is sinking.

It really sucks when that happens. Which were the famous last words of my great-uncle Arden when his sailing ship was caught in a whirlpool.

Chapter Ten

The southern path was, as promised, wide open. We didn't spot a single patrol ship. We had the cannons loaded and stuffed with powder. Our cutlasses were sharp, our eyes sharper. But not one sign of attack. Even the birds veered away from us.

Well, except for one. An hour into our voyage a white dove landed on the ship.

I gave it sunflower seeds out of my pocket. As it pecked from my hand, I unrolled the tiny scroll on its leg. *Where are you? I baked more cookies.*

I began salivating. My dearest, sweetest almost-girlfriend had made me cookies. My heart, if it were not made of muscle, blood and other stuff, would have melted.

I am off to see my father, I wrote back. *Family business. Don't worry. I will enjoy the cookies and hugs when I get back.*

XOXO X

Oh, the last *X* was my signature.

I attached the scroll to the dove, and it flew off. One of the fastest doves I'd ever seen.

Soon Skull Island was in our sights. Dozens of floating zeppelins filled the air, and just as many boats filled the water of the harbor. On the tallest hill on the island stood the royal pirate castle, built of the thickest stone. Dad had designed massive air cannons, hydrogen-seeking rockets and gunpowder balloons that would clear the sky of the enemy for several leagues. Those scurvy Imperial ships wouldn't dare attack.

It was the safest place in the world.

If you're the pirate king, that is. For everyone else, not so much.

We flew in low and came directly to the southern tower. No pirate patrols bothered us—on Dad's orders, I assumed. I handed Bonnie my cutlass, my flintlock and a set of nunchucks that Mrs. Pandora had given me. Oh, and two knuckle-dusters and a mace and three vials of poison. Bonnie was rather loaded down by the time I was done. I felt immensely light.

"You should maybe be taking at least a stiletto in your boot?" she said.

"I trust Dad," I said.

"I be trusting no one," she said. I saw a look in her eyes that might have been kindness. "Except you. I be trusting you, Cap'n."

I nearly teared up. "Get on with you," I said. Then I turned and walked onto the royal dock. I heard Bonnie shout, "Up ship!" I knew that behind me *Cindy* was taking to the skies. I didn't like to see her in the air without me onboard. It did dawn on me I might never see her again.

I strode forward, boots clacking on the bamboo deck. I opened the southern door, which was about a foot thick, and closed and locked it behind me.

The palace is a place stuffed with every treasure from every corner of the world—because every corner of the world sails through our waters and skyways. Tea. Cinnamon. Sugar. Gold ingots. Ancient coffins. Bronze knives. And army sabers. Coins from every nation, even old Empire coins. And about five hundred stuffed parrots.

My dad likes stuffed parrots—he's a collector. It's weird, I know, but pirates are weird.

Dad strolled into the room. He was wearing a white fur robe and purple cloak despite the heat. His golden cutlass was strapped to his waist. His crown, made of golden bones, sat on his head. Whether they are gold-plated real bones or bones made of pure gold, I've never known. Some say they are my uncle's bones.

Like I said, pirates are weird.

"Child number nine," he said. He was never good at remembering our names, especially when he was angry. *Brutus, Clint, Reg, Conn! Get your hands off that saber!* That sort of thing. "Conn!" he added, as my name came to him. He strode directly toward me.

His arms opened wide, and I thought he might be about to put me in a sleeper hold. But before I could react, his arms were around me. It was a hug.

From Dad!

"You must be stressed," he said.

"Just a little. Mom attacked me."

"Oh, did she? I told her not to. But you know your mom."

"And Brutus is dead, and Bartha was—"

He let me go but kept a hand on my shoulder. "Yes. I know all that. Someone is killing us off. One by one. "

"It's not me, Dad." I sounded like a little kid.

"Yes. I know that. You're not smart enough."

"What do you mean?" I spat out.

"Well, it's a complicated plan. To trick Bartha and take her by surprise at her own tree house. To get the Imperial ships to hunt down Brutus. To poison Clint and sabotage Tressa. That takes a lot of planning. And, well, you just don't have the smarts, my son. The know-how. The 'intellect.'" He put that last word in air quotes.

"What do you mean? I'm smart."

"Listen, at least you got my looks. And your mother's stubbornness."

I was smart enough to see this argument was going nowhere.

"I'll prove how smart I am to you later," I said. "But right now I want to know who's behind it all."

"I wanted to bring you back to Skull Island to keep you safe. I have the rest of your remaining siblings in the prison."

"In the prison!"

"Not in the actual prison. Underneath it. In the family safe room. The pirate bunker."

"Really? But I don't want to hide out in a bunker."

"There are cookies."

As if I'd just fall for that.

"Grandma's cookies or Mom's?" I asked. It mattered!

"Grandma's."

Oh, I was so tempted. Grandma makes the best oatmeal-chocolate-chip cookies this side of Oatmeal Island. Mom's, well, she always sneaks ground-up carrots in hers so we won't get scurvy. "I'll think about it."

"There not be a lot of thinking to do, son. In fact, I'll do the thinking from here on in." My father rubbed his beard. "None of your brothers are smart enough either," he said, continuing our previous conversation. "Except Bob. But he's a librarian." Dad spat as if the word was hard to say. "So don't be offended, Conn. A few of your sisters may be smart enough. I just can't figure out which one would do it. Maybe they are working together."

I was still smarting from the "not smart enough" comment. "Listen. I know my ABCs and my numbers. I am smart. Really, really smart."

A white dove landed on the ledge of the barred window nearest to us.

"Who let a dove into the palace?" Dad asked. "I don't like doves. They're judgmental. Unlike parrots."

The dove stared at us. And did appear to be judging us.

"I think it's my—my friend's dove. Her name is Crystal."

"You know someone who likes doves? You should be unfriending that person. Only one person I ever knew liked doves. And she was a horrendously evil person."

"Who?" I asked. I noticed that the dove was making an odd noise. A ticking. *TICK, TICK, TICK*. I wondered if it had a cricket stuck in its throat.

"My sister, your aunt Zeba. She died when you were five."

"I remember the great big explosion. Her whole ship, fifty crew, my little cousin, twelve parrots."

"Yes. And doves. Twelve boxes full of them. Zeba had a thing for doves. But they're horrid creatures." He put his hand on a rope to summon a royal shooer.

TICK, TICK, TICK.

My little toe was starting to tremble. Something was just not right with this dove.

Another dove landed on the windowsill. The bars on the window were meant to keep out invading pirates, ninjas and other enemies. It looked like the bars were close enough together to stop doves from getting in too.

And another white dove landed. Soon there were ten of them.

TICK, TICK, TICK, TICK, they all ticked.

"What the bluebeard blazes?" Dad and I both said at the same time. He owed me a pop.

TICK, TICK, TICK...

BOOOM.

The doves all blew up.

Chapter Eleven

The window was gone. The thick wall of the tower now had a giant hole in it. A hole so large sunlight was streaming in. The room was filled with smoke, dust and the stench of gunpowder.

The doves had been mechanical ticking time bombs. Someone really clever was behind this.

I slowly got up, wiping dust off my breeches. Dad was pulling himself to his feet, using his throne as a handhold.

Several brawny buccaneers came swinging through the smoking hole in the wall, pistols in one hand, rope in the other. That's when I remembered that, thanks to me, the southern path to the castle had been left unguarded.

One of the buccaneers was holding the pickle pirate flag.

Father's eyes widened when he saw the flag.

"It *is* you!" he said. He pointed at me. "You're the traitor."

He staggered toward me. He was so angry he was smoking. Well, it was more likely the smoke was because the blast had lit him on fire.

"It wasn't me!" I said. "I don't know these men."

"Aaaargh!" the buccaneers shouted as they rushed toward us.

Dad drew his cutlass and was about to swing when he collapsed in front of me. I think the force of the blast had just caught up with his brain.

I grabbed his furry smoking cloak and dragged, pulled, heaved and grunted him to the door. The buccaneers were firing shots that pinged off the walls, broke cups and poked holes in stuffed parrots. They mostly missed us except for a zinger through my captain's hat and another that grazed my cheek. Ouch!

I swung open the door and dragged Dad out onto the balcony. I whistled three times.

I know, I know. I was supposed to send my ship out past the perimeter.

I'm a bad son. A bad pirate. Sue me.

Dad thought I was dumb anyway.

Cindy rose up, and her gangplank fell down. Bonnie and Odin helped me drag the king on board before the buccaneers came bursting out of the tower. "Full speed away!" I said.

We did "away" at full speed, but the city guards, not knowing that I was saving Father, began firing at us to protect their king. Cannon shot threatened to smash *Cindy* to splinters. The buccaneers stopped at the edge of the royal tower dock, waving their guns and blades.

The funny thing was, I was pretty certain they could have caught us. But for some reason they stopped. Maybe they were frightened by our guns.

Well, I'd think on that one later. We had some evading to do.

"High-speed evasive maneuvers!" I shouted.

So with flak and fireworks exploding around us, we sailed out of the Pirate

City skies and into the open. The gunfire stopped. We hoisted our camouflage sails, and we were safe.

Well, pirates are never safe.

But we breathed a sigh of relief.

"We be safe and sound," Bonnie said. Then she set about ordering the men to start on the repairs to the ship.

Once they were all gone, I turned to Bonnie. "Do you think I'm smart?" I asked. "I want you to answer truthfully. That's an order."

"That be a tall order," she said. "What be bringing this on?"

"My father said I wasn't smart."

"He be having bad manners. He shouldn't say those things. Even as pirate king."

"But is it true?"

Bonnie didn't shake her head yes or no. She sat there thinking. I was kind of hoping for a faster answer.

"What be your father's words?"

"He said I wasn't smart enough to plan all these attacks. It was really insulting."

"Oh, he be telling the truth then."

"What?" I shouted.

"You be overreacting. You don't have a devious mind. I think that be what he be saying. Plus, you have quick smarts. I'd take those over devious smarts any day."

"Quick smarts?"

"Yep, you solve problems quick like. Lickety-split and all that. Why, lookit how you solved our problems when the ship was on fire. Quick smarts."

I liked the sound of that. I'm not certain that's what Dad was thinking. But I was glad Bonnie thought so highly of me.

"Thanks, Bonnie." I did feel better.

"You be needing your quick smarts right now," she said.

"Why is that? Do you have a problem?"

She pointed up.

"There be a ship above, charging down on us."

Chapter Twelve

She was right. I could see a little black dot growing bigger and bigger.

Coming out of the sun. As I mentioned, it is the oldest trick in the book.

But just as I was about to shout *Open fire!* I hesitated.

The boat had wings and was white as a wedding dress.

Crystal. She was peeking over the edge.

"There you are, Conn! My sweet prince! I am so pleased and happy in my heart that you are safe. I heard guns. And thunder. I was so worried about you."

"Yes, I'm all right," I said. "It has been an adventure. I saved my father from exploding doves and buccaneers in blue. I think the open skies are the best place for him."

"Good thinking. You are so smart." She said this to me face-to-face. How? Because in a heartbeat she'd dropped a rope and rappeled down to the deck of our ship. Impressive feat! Especially in a dress.

She was so beautiful. Like a statue on the front of a ship. But alive. And not made of wood.

"You have no idea how nice that is to hear," I said. I was tempted to make smoochy lips. Maybe this time I'd finally get her to kiss me.

She was holding a second rope that led up to her boat. "You're very smart, Conn. The skies *are* the best place for your father. In fact, why don't we send him up to my boat? No one will look for him there. It's the kind of smart idea you'd think of." She paused. "I have a great pulley system."

"Huh?" I said. But then I realized that didn't sound very smart. "I mean, why would I do that?"

"Because I can take him to Stitch-Me-Up. That's a smart plan. A Conn plan, I should say. He'll be safe there. The kingdom will be safe. I really want to help you out."

I thought about the idea. Bonnie was making some noise, clearing her throat, but I ignored her. Maybe Dad *would* be safer at Stitch-Me-Up.

But something was niggling in the back of my head. A thought. A smart thought. "Why are you doing this?"

"To help you, of course. Friends help each other."

"That is so kind," I said, even though I was thinking I didn't want to be *just* friends. "But I don't think I can send Dad there. The best thing is to find Mom and—"

As I spoke, Crystal's face went dark. "Give. Me. Your. Father!" she shouted. "Right now!" I must say, the look on her face was not attractive. Nor was the spittle that struck my face. It flew like wet shotgun pellets.

"Why are you getting so angry?"

"Give me your father right now. I demand it. So I can finish my revenge."

"What are you talking about? What revenge? You're from Cloud Island. You're always nice."

"No, I'm not. I'm not that at all."
She poked my forehead with her index
finger. "You are so thick-headed."

"Don't say that!" I held my forehead.
"What is with you? You aren't acting
like Crystal at all."

"I'm not Crystal—there is no Crystal.
My name is Betsy. I'm the daughter of
Zeba."

I must admit, I was drawing a blank.
I should have been drawing a gun, but
I was too confused. What the heck was
going on? "Zeba who?"

"Your aunt Zeba. Your mom exploded
her ship."

"Oh. That rings a bell."

"I'm your cousin, you idiot," she
added. "And I'm tenth in line for the
throne." She chuckled. "Sorry, make that
seventh. And now I'm going to kill you."

Chapter Thirteen

"My cousin?" I nearly shouted the word. "But I almost kissed you!"

"It would have been your last kiss."

My brain started to put two and two together. "You're the daughter of Aunt Zeba! Is *she* behind all this?"

"No. Mom's dead. That's why this is revenge. I was on the ship when it crashed. But I didn't die. I climbed out of that wreck, clung onto a chunk of wood and drifted to the Island of the Blue Buccaneers. They raised me and my doves. For the last nine years, I've planned every detail of this brilliant plot to take over the throne. I even faked my way into your school."

"That be a great plan," Bonnie said. She was pointing a flintlock pistol at Crystal—I mean, Betsy. "Except that you be stuck upon our ship."

"Keep your useless king then. I'll just dump you all in the drink." With that, Betsy started hooting like a monkey.

"Stop that!" I said.

"Should I be shooting her?" Bonnie said.

My cousin kept howling and even made a few ape sounds. Then she scratched under her armpits, monkey style.

"I think she's gone mad," I said to Bonnie. "Hold your fire."

Taking advantage of the moment, Betsy shouted toward her boat, "Anchors up!" The white silken rope yanked her up to her boat before Bonnie could get a shot off.

"Enjoy your death by airship!" Betsy shouted down to us.

Her meaning became clear in a few moments. A flock of airships was coming out of the sun. They were small one-person ships, each with a tiny bladder keeping it aloft. I mean tiny in airship terms, of course. So about six yards long.

I didn't believe what I was seeing. The ships were being piloted by monkeys! And each of the little ships had a cannon mounted on the front. The monkeys began firing.

"We be in big trouble now," Bonnie said.

The cannonballs were only the size of oranges, but they shot through the deck just fine. And the monkeys zipped back and forth and stuck with us no matter how we tried to avoid them. No aerial maneuvers would work. The monkey zeppelins were too fast. Soon *Cindy* was a wreck, holes everywhere. A pack of dynamite chucked from a monkey ship blew one of our masts over. It was a miracle that it didn't hit the bladder.

"Give us more power!" I shouted.

But Odin began swearing in another language. In several languages. "A bomb hit the boiler, Captain. She's going to blow!"

"We have to abandon ship," I said. "There is no other way."

"I be going down with the ship," Bonnie said.

"You aren't going down with the ship," I said. "None of us are."

I raced to my cabin and got the bag Mrs. Pandora had given me. The one

I had taken such pains to hide from the crew. Even Bonnie.

"What be these?" she asked.

"Gliding parachutes. I thought it better if the crew didn't know there was a way to escape *Cindy*."

"You be thinking proper," Bonnie said.

"Line the crew up. One by one. I'll take the wheel. You help get the crew off safely."

It took some convincing to get the crew to put on the silky chutes. Then Hooky went over the edge, shouting, "Wheeeeee!" The rest followed. One after the other, dodging the monkey ships and aiming for the nearest island.

"You next!" I said to Bonnie.

"No. I be last off the ship."

"No, the captain is always the last off. Now fly. Like the wind."

"All right, Prince Conn. I be going."

I watched Bonnie slip on the glider. She was over the edge a few seconds later. I heard a faint "Wheeeeee!"

I reached into the bag and pulled out the last glider. Dad and I were the only ones left on the ship. We couldn't use it together. It would rip under our weight. I supposed I could just leave him on the deck. He had called me dumb, after all.

Ah, I couldn't leave him. He'd hugged me! "Dad, Dad!" I said. "Wake up." I splashed some water on his face.

"What is it?"

"Well, we're being attacked by monkeys in airships controlled by your niece Betsy, daughter of Aunt Zeba. She planned all the attacks. Betsy, that is, not Zeba. Aunt Zeba is still dead. The ship is going down, and you need to use this glider parachute to land safely on that island down there. Help is on the way."

"Sounds good, son. Betsy, you say? I never did like that brat."

"Just go!" The monkeys were buzzing all around the ship at this point. Laughing like maniacs.

"What about you?" my father asked.

"I'll be right behind you," I said. Which wasn't exactly a lie. Once he left the ship, I'd be right behind him.

"Good work, son number nine," he said.

He'd forgotten my name again? Jeez. He hugged me again, then pulled on the chute. In seconds he was over the edge. A royal "Wheeee!" soon followed.

"You can't escape me," Betsy called from above. "I'll just sail to the island next." She threw back her head and laughed. "I'm just going to watch your ship go down first."

I waited for my brain to come up with a plan.

And waited.

Speed it up, brain!

A cannonball ripped through the remaining sail. *Cindy* groaned. She was on her last legs. Well, ships don't have legs, but you know what I mean.

Still nothing came. No big idea.

Maybe Dad was right. I wasn't so smart. He could put that on my gravestone. *Conn. At Least He Had His Father's Looks.*

The ship started to fall apart. Along with the last of my self-worth.

Chapter Fourteen

But then it hit me.

Well, actually, a rope hit me. It was one of the moorings that had snapped. It slapped me in the face.

And I got an idea.

I climbed to the top of the crow's nest and then onto the bladder full of hydrogen. One big flaming ball of fire in waiting. Working quickly, I cut the ropes holding the balloon to *Cindy*. I always kept a sharp knife on me.

My dear *Cindy* fell out of the sky with a sigh and several crunching sounds. The monkeys dived after her, perhaps hoping to get one last shot in.

Speaking of shots, without that weight dragging us down, the balloon and I shot up at great speed.

Directly toward Betsy and her stupid swan boat. But it began winging out of the way, and I missed her by a few inches, bumping one edge. "Ha! Missed!" she shouted.

I jumped off the balloon, landed on her ship and drew my blade.

Well, I tried to, but I discovered I had none. But Betsy had her sword and was prepared to use it. Soon I was dancing back and forth on the small boat, ducking and hopping as my cousin did her best to murder me.

I am small. And fast. I dodged and ducked until she stuck the sword into the wooden mast.

"Betsy, stop," I said. "Your plan is finished."

"No!" she shouted and pulled the sword out. She jabbed at me. She missed. I used my quick smarts to come up with a plan. A crazy plan.

I dove over her.

She tried to poke a hole in me, but I twisted in midair, and her blade missed.

And went right into *Swandiver*'s balloon.

You know. The balloon that was keeping us afloat. Hydrogen gas came screaming out, and the ship zigged and zagged, then rocketed up and down. Betsy fell down and bumped her crown.

Hard enough to knock her out.

I managed to cover the hole in the balloon with my hand and guide

Swandiver to the island where all the crew had landed.

Well, not quite to the island. We were about twenty yards short when the ship crashed in the water. I had to drag Betsy to the shore.

My father, Bonnie and my crew helped us once we got out of the water.

The monkeys were gone.

"You did good, son," my father said. "I'm proud of you."

"And so be I," Bonnie said.

I beamed.

Chapter Fifteen

The royal transport ship *Eve* arrived a few hours later, and we were rowed out to her. She was a seafaring vessel, but I didn't hold that against her. Soon we were back at the palace and standing in the partly destroyed throne room. Workers were already patching up the hole caused by the explosions.

y siblings were released from the prison downstairs, and they marched up to see us all.

Reg, the eldest, was first. He gave me a smack on the back that nearly broke my spine. But it was his way of saying, "Good job, bro." They had been told on their way upstairs the story of Dad's rescue. Bartha limped in after Reg and managed to give me a similar smack on the back despite her gut wound. Then Amber and Morgana followed, each winding up and laughing as they slapped my back. I'd have four handprints on my back for the rest of my life.

But it felt good. They were proud of me.

The last to come out was Bob, the librarian. He had his nose in a book and paused only to look me in the eye through his glasses and say, "Epic good work, Conn."

That was a victory all its own. Bob never took his eyes away from a page.

My mom didn't apologize for attacking me. But she did give me a hug and say it was a great escape. That's as close as she comes to apologies.

"Well," I said, about to launch into a speech about how I had won the day.

"Food's here!" Bartha said. And next thing I knew, servers were bringing in smoked turkey, ham, bacon, pork rinds and a tiny plate of fruit.

"Good speech," Dad said. "Keep it short, I always say."

"Thanks," I said. "What's going to happen to Betsy?"

"I have a nice prison cell for her. But she's family, so I won't let her rot. Instead, Bob's going to read books about kindness and politeness to her. It'll drive her crazy. But maybe she'll learn something. And once she does straighten herself out, she'll be free. I am really impressed by her long-term planning. She would make a great general."

I wasn't so certain about the idea of her being in the skies with an armed ship again, but I held my tongue.

"Better grab some grub before it's all gone, son," Dad said.

We ate. We drank. And we managed to avoid the fruit tray.

After we finished saying all our goodbyes, I stood nervously on the bamboo dock, watching for my crew. For my ride.

Finally she rose up. *Cindy 2*. She was bigger, broader, had better guns. But that same old *Cindy* feel.

My father's gift to me.

I stepped on board.

"You be welcome, Captain," Bonnie Brightears said. "Where would you like to go?"

"Let's see where the wind takes us. Sails up!"

"Sails up!" Bonnie repeated.

And we flew.

"Wheeee," I said under my breath.

Arthur Slade is a Governor General's Literary Award–winning author of many novels for young readers, including the graphic novel *Modo: Ember's End*, which is based on characters from *The Hunchback Assignments* trilogy. Raised on a ranch in the Cypress Hills of Saskatchewan, Arthur now makes his home in Saskatoon, Saskatchewan. For more information, visit arthurslade.com.